The Knight and
The Faery Princess

Written by Shirley Tedder

Lived by Slei, the Faery Princess

ACKNOWLEDGMENTS

Thank you!

To all my beloved faery friends who parted the veil and gifted me the true story of why most people no longer see the faery realms. I send you so much love and gratitude.

To all my grandchildren, may you keep the faery magic alive always in your hearts.

Thank you to Patman who never looks at me strangely, no matter what I do. Also, for your help in typing this all out and preparing it for the editor.

I believe in the power and reality of the elemental kingdom. Whilst we believe their magic will always be part of our lives.

Once upon a time of mythical creatures

And tales untold

Of knights on their horses

Daring and bold

Who befriended the pixies, faeries and elves

Who showed them the treasures in nature

That the knights kept for themselves.

Only the knights with purest of heart

Were able to see the magic and beauty

Of the elemental faery

One early morning, the sun bright and warm

The purist young knight arose with the dawn.

He embellished his armor and stood straight and tall,

As he gazed towards the sunrise, he gave thanks for the morn.

Upon his horse he did mount

A day full of wonder ahead you can count

A meeting to take place was in store

It would alter the knight and also much more

A union of human and elemental life,

That would heal physical wounds,

The trouble and strife.

Deep in the forest the faery princess sat,

Her chair was a tree spirit,

Her foot stool a mushroom cap.

Her wings were of gossamer glittering gold

On two stars she made wishes and answers they told.

The peace and healing way

Brought courage to Princess Slei

She deliberated and distressed

That human mankind was in a bad way.

And that healing solutions

Had to be cast that day.

Then suddenly, she felt

An utmost presence rare,

And upon thinking…

The pure knight did appear.

Quindor of Atheon meandered

Through the dappled forest light

His armor shone iridescent bright.

The faery princess ran with grace

And stood with great courage

Before the knight's face.

Their eyes locked together,

A rare union was formed

Filled with love, beauty, devotion,

The mission was born.

A heavenly bond was formed very quick,

To go forth with healing

For humankind's sick.

The faery princess spent

The long-lasting night

Mixing potions of magic dust

Measures just right,

To fill up the pouches

Made from lady slipper purses

To dispel all the darkness

And evil lord curses.

When her work was complete

She hastened to faery King

And kneeled at his feet

To ask for blessings upon the magic dust mix

And protection for the knight Quindor

From the evil lords' tricks

As the dawn did arise

Slei returned to Quindor,

Who was sleeping with tightly shut eyes.

She gently leaned over

And kissed him awake.

He had to arise

His journey to make.

So, the knight ventured forth,

To the corners of the earth

Turning dark into light

Giving humankind back their worth.

Upon returning to his

Faery love's presence.

They would sit through the night and

Relive the journey's essence.

Each mission he made,

Brought more light to the earth,

And with it was heard

Much laughter and mirth.

Mankind was once again

Living with purity of heart

And peace once again reigned

In life it was part.

In a dark corner

That was left on earth

Sat huddled and angry

Were the evil lord herd.

Acknowledging the missions

Were a definite success

They plotted for hours

To bring down the pure knight

And reclaim their dark mess.

So, they waited in patience

And stillness of night

For Quindor to embark

On his last mission

And the bringing down of his plight.

Quindor awoke with Slei in his arms

He loved her so deeply

Her essence so calm.

He knew his last mission

Held dangers intense,

But he had to hold honor

In mankind's defense.

He embellished his armor

And stood straight and tall,

Holding tight in his hands

The last potion for all.

By the light of day's end,

The mission would finish

All dark on the earth

Would completely diminish.

The four elementals

Of earth, air, wind and fire,

Would then live in complete harmony

With humankind and not tire.

The knight Quindor

Bid farewell to his faery princess,

And rode forward

In his best armor and dress.

As he ventured into the last

Darkened corner of night,

As quick as a flash

The pure knight met his plight.

The evil lords lurked

In the dinge and the dark,

And made potions

Of monkshood, hemlock, and larch

To bring down Quindor's protection,

And render him weak,

And give him infection

The outlook was bleak.

The faery princess

Was startled awake

An instant knowing

That was hard to take.

Something surely was very amiss

The light was extinguished

On her eternal bliss.

She sobbed and sighed

And yearned and yearned,

But there was never a sign

Of the knight's return.

The earth and humankind

Relapsed into darkness

The evil lords won

And the light they did harness

To give themselves food

That they were needing

To run one more dark cycle

Initiated from where the knight lay bleeding.

Mankind again fell into

Sickness and strife,

Greed and gluttony

Took over their lives

The king of the faeries

Looked upon his princess daughter,

And for the safety of all elemental beings,

He gave the order.

The elemental kingdoms

Returned to the spirit

And all the amazing treasures

Went along with it.

Unto this day elemental life stays

A vibrational level

Between them and our ways

This is a story of one faery princess

And a love of humankind

With whom she did mesh.

And a knight of pure heart,

Bold, noble, and true

Who took the light to the Earth

Bringing back humankind's worth

All Original Artwork by Shirley Tedder
Check out full portfolio of art and goods on
Facebook.com/dreamweaver-magic-259229277521416

60916495R00015

Made in the USA
Columbia, SC
18 June 2019